KV-589-539

9112000 0395224

BRENT LIBRARIES	
KIL	
91120000395224	
Askews & Holts	20-Feb-2019
JF SHORT CHAPTER	£8.99

Parrots
of the
Caribbean

by Adam Bushnell and Alex Paterson

W
FRANKLIN WATTS
LONDON•SYDNEY

Chapter 1

Once, on a faraway island in the Caribbean, there lived a terrible sea-monster. It had the head of a shark, the body of an electric eel and the claws of a crab. This sea-monster loved nothing more than to eat people. It would slide silently on to land in the dead of night to catch its prey and then slither away again as silently as it had come.

3

It took the people it caught back to its lair
and locked them in a silver cage until
it was hungry.

Then there would be a **munch** ...

and a **crunch** ...

and they were gone!

4

Stories of the strange-looking monster spread far and wide across the kingdom and, although few people had ever seen it, everyone was afraid of the terrible creature.

One dark night, the monster began to feel
hungry again. The silver cage was empty so
the monster slid under the surface of the sea
and swam towards land. Spotting the royal palace
jutting out, not far from the water's edge,
it slithered over the sand and up the high walls.

It slipped in through an open window and captured the sleeping prince. Before the young prince could shout for help, the sea-monster had grabbed him and slid quickly back to the sea. It disappeared under the waves without so much as a splash.

Chapter 2

The next morning, when everyone realised

the prince was missing, there was great panic.

"What will we do?" cried the king.

"Who will find our boy?" sobbed the queen.

Then Sasha, the prince's nanny, stepped forward.

"I know who will help," she said. "The Parrots

of the Caribbean will!"

Everyone turned to look at her.

"Who?" they all gasped

9

"The Parrots of the Caribbean," Sasha said again. "They are the greatest rescue team the world has ever seen. I've heard so many stories about their heroic missions. If anyone can rescue the young prince, they can!"

"What an excellent idea," said the king. "But how can we find them?"

Sasha replied, "It is said that if you ever really need them, you just have to call them. Let's try!"

Sasha stepped towards the window and leaned over.

"Parrots of the Caribbean!" she called out.

"We need you!"

Everyone in the palace held their breath

in anticipation. No one moved. No one spoke.

Then from a distance came the sound of flapping.

It came nearer ... and nearer ... and grew louder

and louder! There was a flutter of feathers, then

in an explosion of colour, four parrots burst

through the open window and into the palace.

"They're here!" Sasha gasped. "The Parrots

of the Caribbean have answered our call!"

13

The four parrots perched on to a table in a line.
The first parrot then flapped its wings in a blur
of colour. "Look! The first is incredibly fast!"
Sasha said, smiling.

The second parrot cupped a wing

over the side of its head.

"Oooh! The second has amazing

hearing!"marvelled the king.

The third parrot flexed its wings.

"The third is extremely strong!" gasped the queen.

The fourth parrot opened its beak and began
to sing. The beautiful melody entranced them.
"The fourth has a voice so beautiful that when
it sings, it can even bring the dead back to life!"
sighed Sasha.

The super fast parrot scanned the room for clues.
Then it zoomed off. Within seconds, it had
returned. In its beak, it held a scale from
an electric eel and the tooth of a shark.
The parrots huddled together and carefully
examined the two mysterious items.

"Do you think you can find the missing prince?" Sasha asked the parrots.

The parrots turned and nodded. This was exactly what they loved to do – rescue those in need! They all looked to the second one in the line. This parrot cupped its wings over its ears and listened carefully. Then, it pointed to the west. The parrots all flew out of the window and were gone.

The super fast parrot led the team as they sped over the sea. Suddenly, they caught sight of a dark, mysterious island. The water reflected the dark, ominous clouds above. As the parrots neared the island, the water swirled and the waves grew to the size of mountains which thrashed and bashed against one another.

Below the gnarled and jagged rocks, the parrots could make out a deep, dark cave. The super fast parrot got there first but the entrance was blocked by a huge boulder. The strong parrot stepped forward. With two punches of its wings, the boulder was reduced to dust.

Chapter 3

The four parrots crouched low and crept into the mouth of the cavernous cave. In the gloom, they heard snoring. The sea monster was sleeping next to the silver cage. The young prince was inside. Slowly and silently, the parrots crept towards him.

The four parrots watched the monster's chest heave up and down, up and down. The snoring was deafening.

The parrot with the beautiful voice began to sing quietly in a slow, melodic lullaby as the monster snored on. The other parrots snatched the keys, unlocked the cage and grabbed the prince. The prince gasped when he saw his rescuers were four parrots!

The extremely strong parrot pointed to its back and the prince jumped on. The parrots sped over the stormy water, back towards the palace. When they reached the beach, the prince jumped down off the back of the strong parrot, relieved.

Just then the parrot with super hearing cupped its feathers around its head. It squawked and pointed across the sea. The sea-monster had woken and was coming this way!

The super fast parrot pointed to a tower on the beach. The prince jumped back on to the extremely strong parrot and they all raced towards the tower. They hid inside and waited in silence. The parrots kept still as statues, not making a flap or a flutter.

The sea-monster rose up from the sea and slithered on to the beach. It stopped and sniffed. It could smell the prince's fear. It smashed the top off the tower with its crab's claws. Then it reached inside and grabbed the prince before swiftly slithering towards the sea.

Quickly, the extremely strong parrot lifted up a massive boulder and hurled it towards the monster.

The sea monster fell to the ground ... dead.

The extremely strong parrot rolled the boulder
to one side. The sea-monster lay flat on its back,
not moving. But to the parrots' horror, the boulder
that had crushed the sea monster had also
squashed the prince!

Was he alive? Was he breathing?

The parrot with the beautiful voice stepped forward.

The three parrots held their breath as the fourth parrot opened its beak and began to sing ...
Its song was so beautiful that the prince slowly started to murmur. Then he sat up. Then he stood up. He was alive! The parrots all squawked with joy. Happily, they set off toward the palace with the prince.

The king and queen were delighted. They threw a party to celebrate the prince's safe return. The parrots proudly told the guests the story of their daring rescue. The king presented each of the parrots with medals for their bravery.

Meanwhile, far across the sea, something was stirring. When the singing parrot had sung his magical song, it had brought the prince back to life … but it had also reawakened the sea-monster! Slowly, it slithered into the water and swam back toward its island in the sea. There was no doubt he would be meeting the Parrots of the Caribbean again one day …

Things to think about

1. What features does the sea-monster have? Is it like any other mythical monsters you have read about?
2. Why does the sea-monster kidnap the prince?
3. Who comes to the rescue and whose idea is it to call them?
4. What distinguishing feature does each parrot have? How do they work as a team to rescue the prince?
5. What do you think about the ending?

Write it yourself

This story is about the defeat of a monster. Now try to write your own story about a monster and how it was overcome. Plan your story before you begin to write it. Start off with a story map:

• a beginning to introduce the characters and where and when your story is set (the setting);

• a problem which the main characters will need to fix in the story;

• an ending where the problems are resolved.

Get writing! Think about using an exotic mythical setting and how you might set the scene with gripping descriptions and alliteration.

Notes for parents and carers

Independent reading

The aim of independent reading is to read this book with ease. This series is designed to provide an opportunity for your child to read for pleasure and enjoyment. These notes are written for you to help your child make the most of this book.

About the book

Once there lived a terrible sea-monster who abducted a young prince for its dinner. Luckily, the prince's nanny knows just who to call for help: a team of monster-bashing experts known as the Parrots of the Caribbean!

Before reading

Ask your child why they have selected this book. Look at the title and blurb together. What do they think it will be about? Do they think they will like it?

During reading

Encourage your child to read independently. If they get stuck on a longer word, remind them that they can find syllable chunks that can be sounded out from left to right. They can also read on in the sentence and think about what would make sense.

After reading

Support comprehension by talking about the story. What happened?
Then help your child think about the messages in the book that go beyond the story, using the questions on the page opposite. Give your child a chance to respond to the story, asking:
Did you enjoy the story and why? Who was your favourite character?
What was your favourite part? What did you expect to happen at the end?

Franklin Watts
First published in Great Britain in 2019
by The Watts Publishing Group

Copyright © The Watts Publishing Group 2019
All rights reserved.

Series Editors: Jackie Hamley and Melanie Palmer
Series Advisors: Dr Sue Bodman and Glen Franklin
Series Designer: Peter Scoulding

A CIP catalogue record for this book is
available from the British Library.

ISBN 978 1 4451 6246 1 (hbk)
ISBN 978 1 4451 6331 4 (pbk)
ISBN 978 1 4451 6330 7 (library ebook)

Printed in China

Franklin Watts
An imprint of
Hachette Children's Group
Part of The Watts Publishing Group
Carmelite House
50 Victoria Embankment
London EC4Y 0DZ

An Hachette UK Company
www.hachette.co.uk

www.franklinwatts.co.uk

FSC
www.fsc.org
MIX
Paper from
responsible sources
FSC® C104740